מסורה

ArtScroll Youth Series ®

This book
belongs to:

_____

_____

Published by Mesorah Publications, ltd

ALEF

Written by Yaffa Ganz

Illustrated by Michael Horen

Typography & design by Rabbi Sheah Brander

For Bezalel and Yair

both of whom are using

the letters of the alef-beit

to build worlds of Torah

for Klal Yisrael.

הָעוֹלָם נִבְרָא בִּלְשׁוֹן הַקּוֹדֶשׁ.

The world was created with Hebrew, the language of holiness. *Midrash* / ב״ר לא:ח

FIRST EDITION
Nine Impressions . . . February 1989 — June 2006
Tenth Impression . . . November 2009

Published and Distributed by
MESORAH PUBLICATIONS, Ltd.
4401 Second Avenue
Brooklyn, New York 11232

Distributed in Europe by
LEHMANNS
Unit E, Viking Business Park
Rolling Mill Road
Jarrow, Tyne & Wear NE32 3DP
England

Distributed in Australia & New Zealand by
GOLDS WORLD OF JUDAICA
3-13 William Street
Balaclava, Melbourne 3183
Victoria Australia

Distributed in Israel by
SIFRIATI / A. GITLER — BOOKS
6 Hayarkon Street
Bnei Brak 51127

Distributed in South Africa by
KOLLEL BOOKSHOP
Ivy Common 105 William Road
Norwood 2192, Johannesburg, South Africa

THE ARTSCROLL YOUTH SERIES®
ALEF TO TAV
© *Copyright 1989, 2006 by* MESORAH PUBLICATIONS, Ltd. *and* YAFFA GANZ
4401 Second Avenue / Brooklyn, N.Y. 11232 / (718) 921-9000 / www.artscroll.com

ISBN 10: 0-89906-962-2 / ISBN 13: 978-0-89906-962-3 (hard cover)
ISBN 10: 0-89906-963-0 / ISBN 13: 978-0-89906-963-0 (paperback)

Typography by CompuScribe at ArtScroll Studios, Ltd.
4401 Second Avenue / Brooklyn, N.Y. 11232 / (718) 921-9000

Printed in Canada

ד ג ב א

ט ח ז ו ה

נ מ ל כ י

ס ע פ צ ק

ק ר ש ת

$$1 = א$$

א אוֹ אָ אַ אֶ
אֶ אָ אוֹ אִ אֵ

אָלֶף ALEF

אַשְׁרֵינוּ מַה טוֹב חֶלְקֵנוּ וּמַה נָּעִים גּוֹרָלֵנוּ וּמַה יָּפָה יְרֻשָּׁתֵנוּ.

How fortunate we are! How good is our portion, how pleasant our lot, and how beautiful our heritage. *Prayer Book* / סידור

אַרְיֵה	אֶתְרֹג	אֹזֶן
aryeh	esrog/etrog	ozen

lion

esrog/etrog

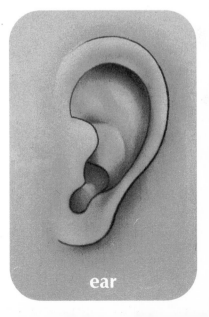

ear

One *abba*, one *imma*, two *achim*, and three *achayos/achayot*
make a family of seven.

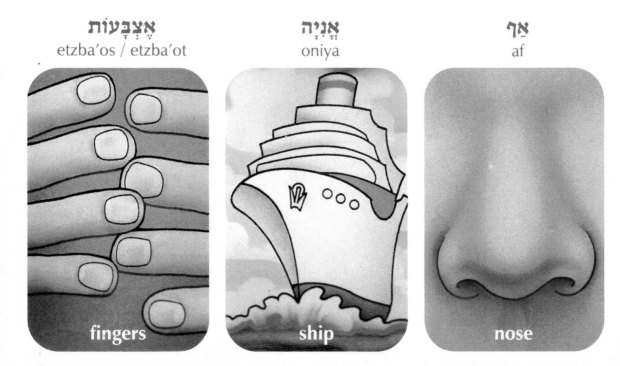

אֶצְבָּעוֹת
etzba'os / etzba'ot

fingers

אֳנִיָּה
oniya

ship

אַף
af

nose

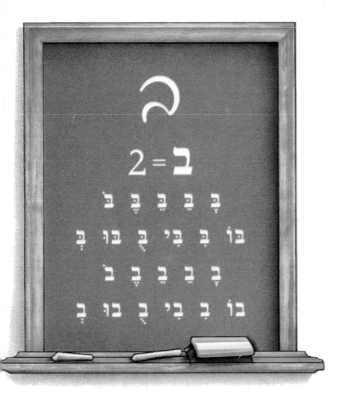

בֵּית BEIS / BEIT

בְּרֵאשִׁית בָּרָא אֱלֹקִים אֵת הַשָּׁמַיִם וְאֵת הָאָרֶץ.

In the beginning, G-d created the heavens and the earth. *Genesis* 1:1 בראשית

בַּיִת
bayis/bayit

בֵּיצָה
beytza

בָּקָר
bakar

house

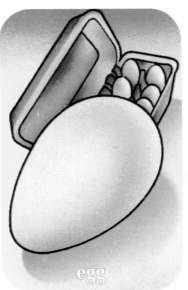

egg

cattle

Binyamin is bringing a basketful of *bikkurim* to the *Beis/Beit Hamikdash*.

בַּר מִצְוָה
bar mitzvah

bar mitzvah

בְּשָׂמִים
besamim

spices

בַּרְוָז
barvaz

duck

3 = גּ

גּ גּ גּ גּ

גּוֹ גִּי גַּ גּוּ גָּ

גִּימֶל GIMMEL

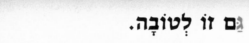

גַּם זוֹ לְטוֹבָה.

This, too, is only for the good. *Talmud* תענית כא

גְּפָנִים	גְּלִידָה	גְּדִי
gefanim	gelida	gedi

grape vines

ice cream

baby goat

Oops! Gershon almost forgot to make the *beracha "borei peri hagafen"* before gulping down that glass of grape juice.

גָּמָל	גֶּשֶׁר	גֶּשֶׁם
gamal	gesher	geshem

camel

bridge

rain

4 = דַ

דָ דַ דֶ דְ דֵ

דוֹ דֻ דִי דֹ דוּ דַ

DALET דָלֶת

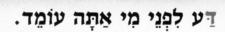

דַע לִפְנֵי מִי אַתָּה עוֹמֵד.

Know before Whom you are standing. *The Tzava'a of Rebbi Eliezer Hagadol*

דֻבְדְבָן	דְלִי	דָג
duvdevon	deli	dag

cherry

pail

fish

This poor *dov* went looking for *devash* but he found a *devora* instead!

דֶּקֶל	דַּחְלִיל	דֶּגֶל
dekel	dachlil	degel

palm tree

scarecrow

flag

ה = 5

הָ הַ הֵ הֹ הוֹ הֹ
הִי הַ הוּ הַ הָ הֵ

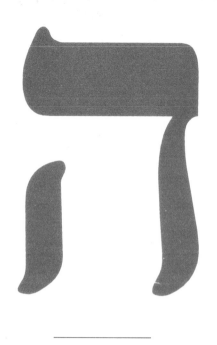

הֵא HEY

הֱוֵי מְקַבֵּל אֶת כָּל הָאָדָם בְּסֵבֶר פָּנִים יָפוֹת.

Greet every person with a smile. *Ethics of the Fathers* 1:15 פרקי אבות

הַגָּדָה
haggada

הַרְמוֹנִיקָה
harmonika

הַס
haas!

haggada

harmonica

shhh!

If Hillel doesn't turn the *hegeh* quickly, he's going to hit that helicopter.

הֲדַס	הַבְדָּלָה	הַר
hadas	havdala	har

myrtle

havdala

mountain

וּ = 6

וָ וֵ וִ וֹ וּ
וָ וִ וֹ וּ
וֵ וֹ וּ וְ

וָו VAV

Queen Vashti had a *vikuach* with King Achashveyrosh, and was she ever sorry!

וְאָהַבְתָּ לְרֵעֲךָ כָּמוֹךָ.

You shall love your neighbor as much as you love yourself.

Leviticus 19:18 ויקרא

וִילוֹן
vilon

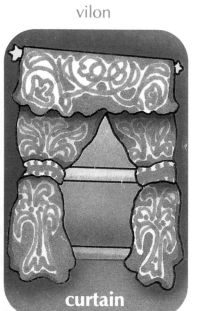

curtain

וֶרֶד
vered

rose

וָו
vahv

hook

ז = 7

זַ זַ זְ זֹ

זוֹ זִ זִי

זֶ זוּ זָ

ZAYIN זַיִן

A *zakeyn* with a long *zakan* riding on a zippy *zehbra*.

זָכוֹר אֶת יוֹם הַשַּׁבָּת לְקַדְּשׁוֹ.

Remember the Sabbath, to keep it holy. *Exodus* 20:8 שמות

זַיִת
zayis/zayit

זָהָב
zahav

זְאֵב
z'ev

olive

gold

wolf

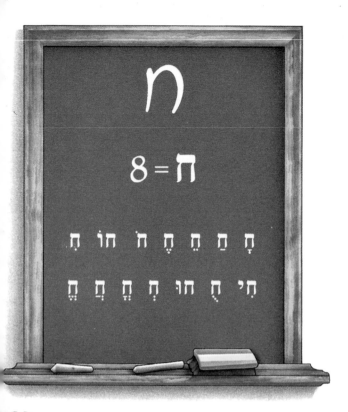

ח = 8

CHES / CHET חֵית

חֲבֵרִים כָּל יִשְׂרָאֵל.

All Jews are united as brothers and friends. *Prayer Book* / סידור

חֻלְצָה
chultza

חִטָּה
chitta

חָתוּל
chasul/chatul

shirt

wheat

cat

מַזָל טוב

The *chassan/chattan* is standing under the *chuppa* waiting for the *kallah*

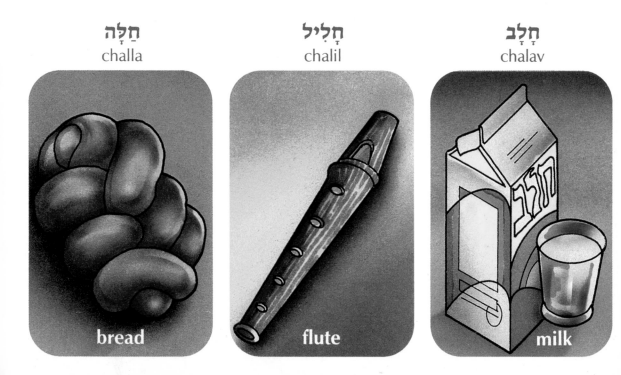

חַלָה	חָלִיל	חָלָב
challa	chalil	chalav
bread	flute	milk

$$ט = 9$$

טָ טַ טָ טַ

טוֹ טְ טִי טַ טוּ טְ

TES / TET טֵית

טוֹב לִי תוֹרַת פִּיךָ מֵאַלְפֵי זָהָב וָכָסֶף.

The words of Your Torah are dearer to me
than thousands of pieces of gold and silver. *Psalms* 119:72 תהלים

טַבַּעַת	טַיָּס	טָלֶה
taba'as/taba'at	tayas	taleh

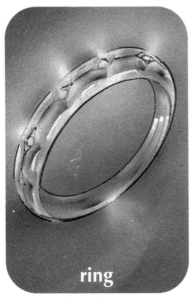

ring

pilot

sheep

Um . . . the *tabach* added one more tiny *tipa* of something tasty
into the soup and the *ta'am* was just perfect!

טַלִּית
tallis/tallit

טֶלֶפוֹן
telefone

טַוַּס
tavas

tallis/tallit

telephone

peacock

YUD יוּד

יָפֶה תַלְמוּד תּוֹרָה עִם דֶּרֶךְ אֶרֶץ.

It is good to combine the study of Torah with
a means of earning a livelihood. *Ethics of the Fathers* 2:2 פרקי אבות

יָם
yam

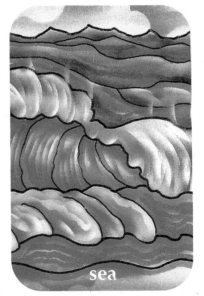

sea

יַיִן
yayin

wine

יֶלֶד
yeled

boy

Yareyach over Yerushalayim.

יָד
yad

יַנְשׁוּף
yanshuf

יַלְדָּה
yalda

hand

owl

girl

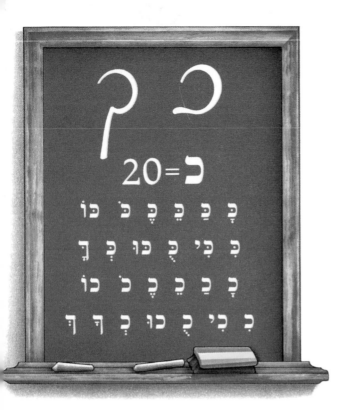

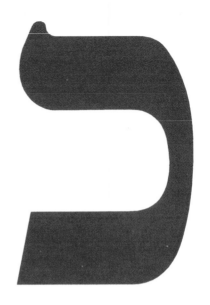

$20 = $ כ

KAF כָּף

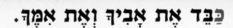

כַּבֵּד אֶת אָבִיךָ וְאֶת אִמֶּךָ.

You shall honor your father and your mother. *Exodus* 20:12 שמות

כֵּסֵא	כֹּהֵן גָדוֹל	כּוֹתֶל
kisay	kohen gadol	kosel/kotel

chair

kohen gadol

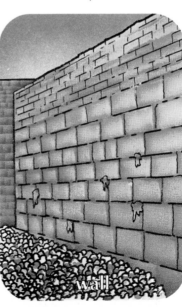

wall

Here comes the *kallah*. She's wearing a *keser/keter* made out of *kesef* on her head and she looks just like a queen!

כּוֹבַע
kova

כֶּלֶב
kelev

כַּדוּר
kadur

hat

dog

ball

ל = 30

לֶ לַ לֵ לִ

לוֹ לְ לִי לֵ לוּ לֹ

לָמֶד LAMED

לְשָׁנָה הַבָּאָה בִּירוּשָׁלַיִם!

Next year, may we be in Jerusalem! *Passover Haggada* / הגדה של פסח

לְבִיבוֹת
levivos/levivot

לַיְלָה
layla

לֶחֶם
lechem

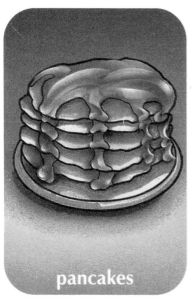

pancakes

night

bread

Levi is all confused. He took a *lulav* to a *Lag Ba'Omer* picnic!

לוּל
lule

playpen

לְטָאָה
leta'a

lizard

לוּחַ
luach

calendar

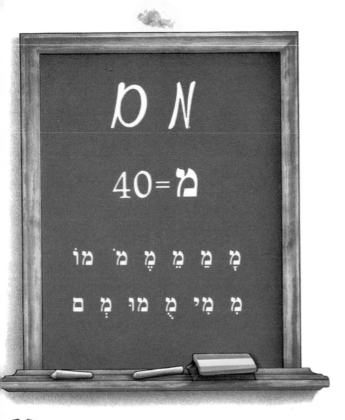

מ = 40

מוֹ מֶ מַ מֻ מָ

מֶם מוּ מִי מְ

מֵם **MEM**

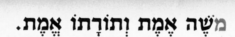

מֹשֶׁה אֱמֶת וְתוֹרָתוֹ אֱמֶת.

Moshe is true and his Torah is true. *Midrash* / מדרש תנחומא

מִכְנָסַיִם	מַצָּה	מְאַוְרֵר
michnasayim	matza	m'avrer

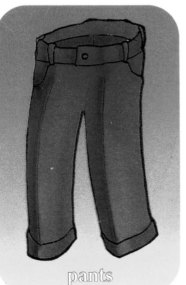

pants

matza

fan

This *mishpacha* is very busy with an important *mitzva*.
They are putting a *mezuza* on every doorpost in their new mansion.

מִסְפָּרַיִם
misparayim

מָטוֹס
matos

מַזְלֵג
mazleg

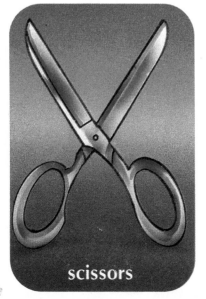

scissors

airplane

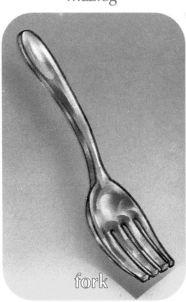

fork

50 = ב

נוֹ בׁ נְ נַ
ן. נׇ נוּ נׅ בִּי בּ

נוּן NUN

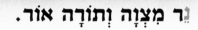

נֵר מִצְוָה וְתוֹרָה אוֹר.

The performance of a mitzva is like light from a candle;
learning Torah is like light from the sun. *Proverbs* 6:23 משלי

נוֹצָה	נַעַל	נַדְנֵדָה
notza	na'al	nadneyda

feather

shoe

swing

A ferocious *nahmer*, a long, stringy *nachash*, and an itsy bitsy *nemalah*, all napping in the noonday sun.

נְטִילַת יָדַיִם
netilas/netilat yadayim

נֶבֶל
nevel

נֵר
ner

washing the hands

harp

candle

SAMECH סָמֶךְ

סוּר מֵרָע וַעֲשֵׂה טוֹב.

Turn away from evil and do only good. *Psalms* 34:15 תהלים

סַל
sal

סֵפֶר
sefer

סוֹפֵר
sofer

basket

book

scribe

Bring another *safsal* into the *sukkah*
so there's enough sitting space for everyone!

סוּס	סֵפֶל	סַפָּר
suse	seyfel	sapar

horse

cup

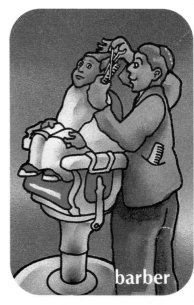

barber

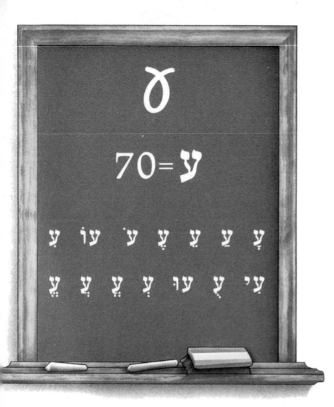

70 = עַ

עַ עַ עַ עוּ עַ

עִי עַ עוּ עָ עָ

AYIN עַיִן

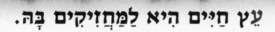

עֵץ חַיִּים הִיא לַמַּחֲזִיקִים בָּהּ.

The Torah is a Tree of Life
to those who follow its commandments. *Proverbs 3:18* משלי

עֲצֹר!	עֲשֶׂרֶת הַדִּבְּרוֹת	עַיִן
Atzor!	aseres hadibros/aseret hadibrot	ayin

stop sign

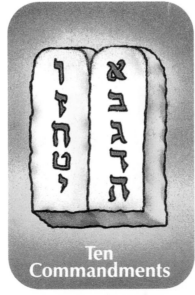

Ten
Commandments

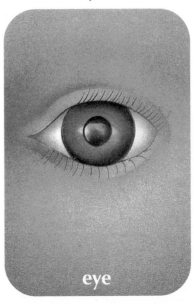

eye

An *achbar* ate the *oogah* Aliza had baked.

עִפָּרוֹן	עַכָּבִישׁ	עֲפִיפוֹן
eeparon	akavish	afifon
pencil	spider	kite

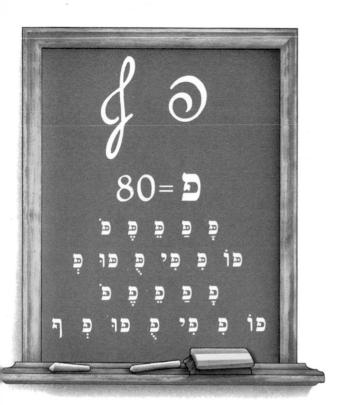

PEY פֵּא

פּוֹתֵחַ אֶת יָדֶךָ וּמַשְׂבִּיעַ לְכָל חַי רָצוֹן.

You open Your hand and satisfy the wishes of
every living creature. *Psalms* 145:16 תהלים

פַּרְפַּר	פֵּרוֹת	פֶּה
parpar	peyros/peyrot	peh

butterfly

fruit

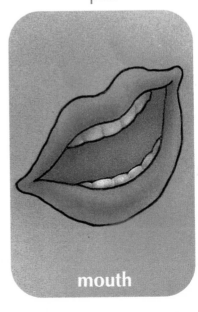

mouth

A rather plumpish *peel* ringing a *pa'amon* and playing the *p'santer*.

פֶּרַח
perach

flower

פַּטִּישׁ
patish

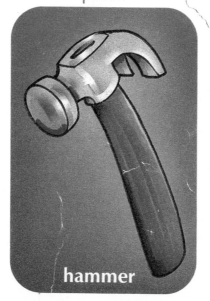

hammer

פַּרְדֵּס
pardes

orchard

90 = צ

צַ צֵ צֻ צוֹ

צִי צְ צוּ ץ

צָדִי TZADI

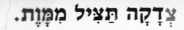

צְדָקָה תַּצִּיל מִמָּוֶת.

Giving charity will lengthen the years of your life. *Proverbs* 10:2 משלי

צְפַרְדֵּעַ
tzefardeya

צְדָקָה
tzedaka

צִיצִית
tzitzis/tzitzit

frog

charity

tzitzis/tzitzis

The *tzalam* is taking a picture of Tzippora's long *tzama*.

צְנוֹן
tzenohn

raddish

צִפּוֹר
tzipor

bird

צוֹלֶלֶת
tzolleles/tzollelet

submarine

100=ק

ק ק ק ק ק
ק קִי קִ קוּ קֵ
ק קוּ קִי קֵי קֻ

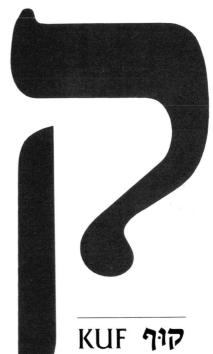

קוּף KUF

קָדוֹשׁ קָדוֹשׁ קָדוֹשׁ ה׳ צְבָקוֹת מְלֹא כָל הָאָרֶץ כְּבוֹדוֹ.

Holy, holy, holy, is Hashem, Master of Hosts.
The whole world is filled with His glory. *Isaiah 6:3* ישעיה

קָלָב
kolav

קוּמְקוּם
kumkum

קִדוּשׁ
kiddush

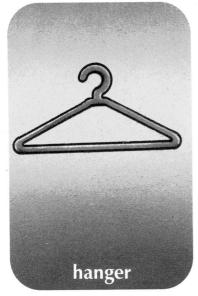

hanger

teapot

kiddush

When Noach came out of the Ark and offered a *korban* to Hashem,
he saw a *keshes/keshet* in the sky.

קוֹף
kof

קוּר
koor

קִפּוֹד
kipode

monkey

spider's web

porcupine

200 = ר

רָ רַ רֶ ר

רוֹ רְ רִי רָ רוּ רֶ

רֵישׁ RESH

רֵאשִׁית חָכְמָה יִרְאַת ה'.

The fear of Hashem is the beginning of wisdom. *Psalms* 111:10 תהלים

רִמּוֹן	רוֹכְסָן	רַכֶּבֶת
rimon	rochsan	rakeves/rakevet

pomegranate

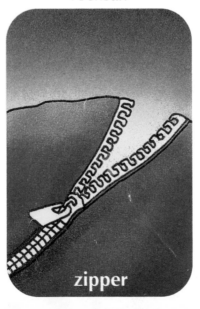

zipper

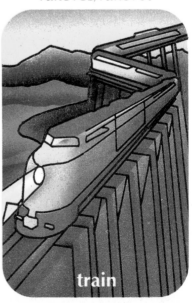

train

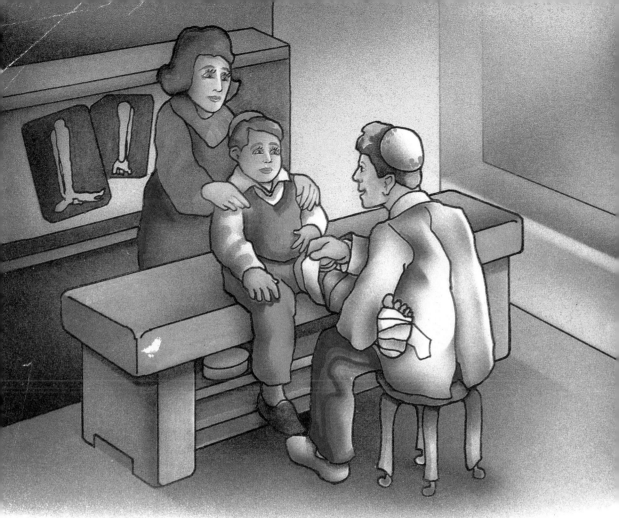

When Reuven tripped on a rock and broke his *regel*,
his mother took him straight to the *rofey*.

רְאִי
r'ee

רֶפֶת
refes/refet

רֶגֶל
regel

mirror

barn

foot

300 = שׁ

שׁוּ שַׁ שֶׁ שֵׁ שַׁ שְׁ שֶׁ שׁוּ
שַׁ שׁוּ שׁוּ שִׁי שַׁ שֶׁ
שׁוּ שֵׁ שֶׁ שֵׁ שַׁ שׁוּ
שׁוּ שִׁי שַׁ שֶׁ שׁוּ שֵׁ

שִׁין SIN   שִׁין SHIN

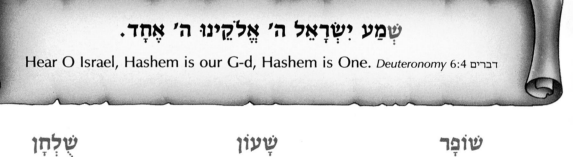

שְׁמַע יִשְׂרָאֵל ה' אֱלֹקֵינוּ ה' אֶחָד.

Hear O Israel, Hashem is our G-d, Hashem is One. *Deuteronomy* 6:4 דברים

שֻׁלְחָן	שָׁעוֹן	שׁוֹפָר
shulchan	sha'ohn	shofar

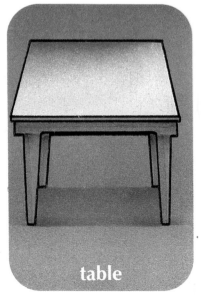

table

clock

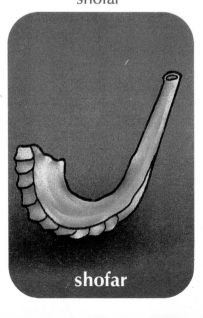

shofar

Seven days make a *shavua* —
six days of work and one day for *Shabbos/Shabbat*.

שָׁמַיִם
shamayim

heaven

שִׁנַּיִם
sheenayim

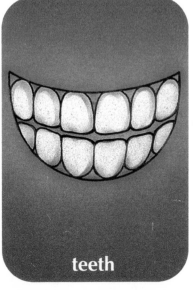
teeth

שׁוּעָל
shu'al

fox

ת

ת = 400

תָ תַ תֶ תָ ת
תּוּ תִי תָ תּוּ ת
תָ תֶ תַ ת
תּוּ ת תִי ת תּוּ ת

תָּו TAV

תּוֹרָה צִוָּה לָנוּ מֹשֶׁה מוֹרָשָׁה קְהִלַּת יַעֲקֹב.

Moshe commanded us to keep the Torah.
It is an inheritance for the Jewish people. *Deuteronomy* 33:4 דברים

תַּרְנְגוֹל	תַּפּוּחַ	תְּאֵנָה
tarnegol	tapuach	t'eyna

rooster

apple

fig

There once was a *tinok* who was put in a *teyvah*.
A long time later — eighty years! — Hashem taught him the *Torah*!

תֹּף
tof

תַּפּוּז
tapuz

תְּפִילִין
tefillin

drum

orange

tefillin

This volume is part of the
ArtScroll Youth Series®
books especially written and designed for
the younger reader.

ArtScroll Middos Books — in which the very young learn by watching those with good *middos* and saying, "I want to be like that!" And by watching those without good *middos* and saying, "Oh no! I don't want to be like that!" With full-color illustrations on every page.

ArtScroll Junior Classics — in which the very young learn chapters of our history and pages from the Talmud and Midrash; with full color illustrations on every page.

Stories — true and imagined; from every land in which Jews have lived, and from every era; including fully illustrated books for all ages from pre-school to late teen.

Biography and History — the lives and times of many of the greatest Torah leaders of the past four centuries; written and illustrated for the early teenager.

Scripture and Liturgy — *Megillas Esther,* the *Haggadah, Pirkei Avos;* all with complete Hebrew text, a translation and commentary written with the pre-teen in mind, and full-color illustrations.

For a brochure of current publications
visit your local Hebrew bookseller
or contact the publisher:

Mesorah Publications, Ltd.
4401 Second Avenue
Brooklyn, New York 11232
(718) 921-9000
www.artscroll.com